THE CAVE OF SANTA CLOPS

WRITTEN AND DRAWN

BY

GIG WAILGUM

© 2014

WAILGUM ART YARNS

To Clement Clarke Moore, Theodor Seuss Geisel and
Sir Ernest Henry Shackleton,

as well as James, John, Jennifer and my parents

ISBN-13: 978-1502365903
ISBN-10: 1502365901
LCCN: 2014917257
BISAC: Juvenile Fiction / Holidays & Celebrations / Christmas & Advent

'Twas a sight before Christmas,
and all over town,
wintry white snow
had just fallen down.

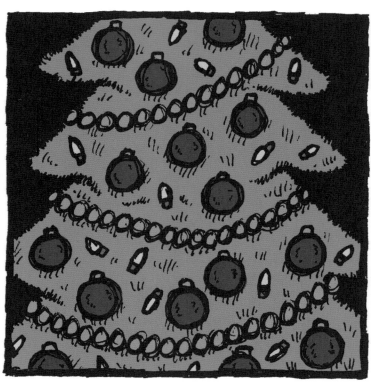

The stockings were hung. The trees were cloaked.

The gifts were wrapped, and the kids were stoked!

Tristan and his sister Rose were quite excited too.
Indeed, Christmas was coming; tomorrow it was due.

They had just read the *Visit From Santa Clops* book,
a fun yuletide yarn, that's certainly worth a look. ;-)

Is there a Santa Clops?

they asked, as most children do.

I don't know, said their mom.

but Mr. Bones says it's true.

Tristan and Rose piled on their clothes and ran out in a hurry!
After building a fortress, the missiles flew in a flurry.

They ran about the yard chucking snowballs around,
one throw missed its mark, but another it found.

Tristan's toss topped
Mr. Ody Bone's crown,
which knocked the old gent
right to the ground.

After Ody got to his feet, Tris said,

Sorry mister, I wasn't aiming for you, just my little sister.

Just aiming for your sister? Boy, you'd best behave. Santa Clops is coming! He's leaving his cave!

If you don't want a lump of coal in your stocking, you'd better not act so wild and shocking.

Come on, Mr. Bones, is Santa Clops really real?

Tristan and his sister still weren't sure of that deal.

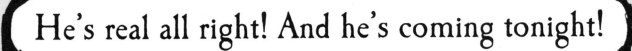

He's real all right! And he's coming tonight!

thundered Ody with added might.

How are you so sure about this?

questioned a curious Tris.

Well, if you have some time, I will tell you the tale of my night in his cave during a South Pole gale.

Tristan and little Rose wanted to know.
So they plunked right down and sat in the snow.

Odysseus Bones fixed his hat and coat,
brushed off some snow, and cleared his throat.

I will tell you two children
all I can remember
of that dark and stormy
Antarctic December.

There I was, a young lad, some sixty-odd years ago, way down under in the land of ice and snow.

I was there with my parents who were part of a big team, studying Antarctica was their scientific dream.

Now December at the South Pole is actually summer. But it's not quite beach weather, which isn't a bummer.

The sun hardly sets, so there's extra daylight, which gives the impression of having no night.

It's warmer than winter, and there's still ice and snow. But at least it's not a hundred below!

Now at the time, I had made a super secret goal, to have a Christmas adventure at the South Pole.

Earlier my parents had warned not to go off alone, on any exploring outside the camp safety zone.

Stubborn of mind, I wrongly decided to go. Even if my folks had emphatically said "no."

The weather was fine, that day I snuck off on my quest. It was Christmas Eve and I skied without rest.

My feet were getting cold and my nose was turning blue.
I felt my Christmas wish would never come true.

I had to find some shelter so I could get warm.
It was the only way I'd survive that awful storm.

Up ahead, on a hill, I saw a cave,
there I skied, for my life I had to save.

When I finally staggered in and took a good look,
the entrance slammed shut like a granite book!

I tried to go back out, the way in which I came,
but those big rocky doors stayed shut just the same.

Down the tunnel I spotted a dim light.
Was this the way out? An end to my plight?

My only choice was to go deep into that craggy cave.
It was extremely spooky, but I was feeling brave.

After walking for a while, I heard some talking,
in voices that sounded like two turkeys squawking.

I quickly ducked behind a nearby boulder,
and took a gander back over my shoulder.

My eyes and ears were shocked at what they saw and heard.
Two giant walking, talking, dino-penguin birds!

I must be dreaming!

I puzzled and thought.

How can penguins speak?
I thought they could not!

And look at their heads! They're shaped like picks!
They look like tuxedoed, pterodactyl chicks!

I trailed the pick-headed birds and saw strange sights that day,
in the twisting tunnels that went every which way.

Mining took place in many rocky alleys and shafts;
in one burrow I saw young penguins learning their craft.

The feisty birds peck and chip on stone with their beak;
I wanted to stay and watch, but could only peek.

I stuck with the two waddlers as they went along the burrow.
Then we came upon a room that made my brow furrow.

Hung from stalactites was a peculiar moving picture screen.
It was made of ice and electronics like I'd never seen.

The screen showed films of children doing naughty things.
And beside it a list of names was issuing.

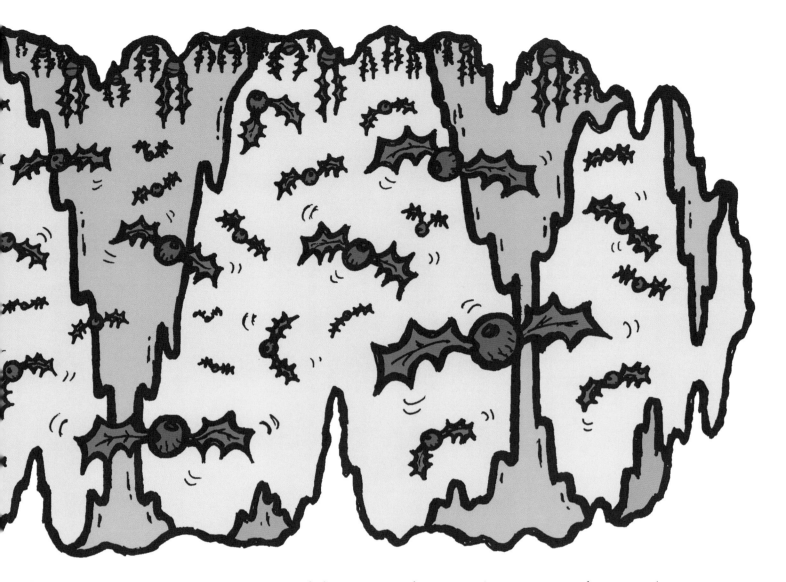

Above it all, a colony of bizarre bats clung to the ceiling.
Their eyeball bodies and holly-leaf wings gave me a creepy feeling.

The holly-bats constantly came and went from the room.
The quivering group looked like a festering plume.

Those that came in went to the device in the center.
And the screen would change, as if a film had been entered.

I didn't look long because the birds had left.
So I crept off to catch up, quickly and deft.

I shadowed the birds till we came to a large hall,
in which sat a sleigh that was curiously oddball.

The front of it was normal, with a seat at the head,
but the back was a dump truck, with a tilting bed.

The massive vessel stood on lengthy wooden skis,
which would allow it to slide on snow with ease.

The sleigh sort of copied the one from the North Pole,
except for the truck part, which was filled with coal.

I heard many voices coming and needed to hide.
The only place was the sleigh, so I hid just beside.

I peeked over the pile to see who it was,
and saw many penguins. The cave was abuzz!

Then the cavern went silent, no longer a noisy din.
I could not see much, but someone had walked in.

From the rear, I saw his red coat and hat.
He was big and stocky, but not very fat.

I thought, sitting there in hiding, "This must be a trick!
Do my eyes deceive me? Is that the back of Saint Nick?"

He spoke not a word. He just pointed his mitten about.
Each penguin he selected let out a happy shout.

Yippy! Hurray!
The master picked me!
Tonight I will fly over
land and sea!

The man in red gave each
of the chosen a candy fish.
They swallowed the sweets
and recited a little wish.

A fish, a wish,
to fly so high.
Cross my heart
and wink an eye.

While the lucky ones were hitched to the front of the sleigh,

the other birds stepped back and cleared a runway.

I had to duck down when he climbed in the sled, so I still had not seen the front of his head.

Then I found one of the candy fish by my feet. It must have fallen there when he got in his seat.

The big Santa grabbed the reins and the sleigh bells jingled. The cave was a-rockin' and my backbone tingled!

My birds,

he gravely said,

You dug the coal and loaded it too. You have eaten the magic fish. Now do what seagulls do!

Just before he spoke, I stuffed the fish in my pocket. Good thing I did because we took off like a rocket!

With my feet on the ski, I gripped the dumper-bed, I held on for dear life, and ducked my head.

We blasted through the cave in a twisting, dark tunnel. It was like flying inside a tornado-funnel!

Soon we were out in the cold polar air.
The storm had stopped and the weather was fair.

Below in the snow, I spotted the South Pole.
I was so happy I knocked off some coal.

That's when he spun around and gave me a look,
a look to this day, I never have shook!

From the moment I saw it, I thought I might die, for the face of this Santa, had only ONE EYE!

In fright I jumped back and fell off the sleigh.
To earth I was falling! Was this my last day?

Then I remembered the magic little fish.
I swallowed it quick and shouted the wish.

It was then that I felt what birds do all day,
that feeling of flight, was more than okay!

Like a super hero, I soared through the air!
I steered with my arms, the wind in my hair!

But the Cyclops had turned back to get me.
Ready for battle, I had to be.

I flew up, and then down, and landed near the Pole.
Then I searched the sky for that red-coated troll.

Santa Clops and his sled flew right over my head.
He threw some black snow and I prayed,

I tried to fly again,
jumping up from the snow,
but the Clops' black powder
made it a no-go.

The myths of old say Cyclops
eat men and much more.
Was this what the one-eyed beast,
for me, had in store?

Again the sleigh circled back in the gloomy twilight.
Was I to be dinner? I hoped that wasn't right.

But then it was quite clear, there was nothing to fear.

Scary Christmas!

he shouted,

And Happy
New Year!

As they sped off to the north,
the last thing I heard,
was the Clops' warning,

Heed your
parents' words!

And that's how he left me, on top of a snowy knoll, standing on Christmas Day at the great South Pole.

In an unexpected way my holiday wish had come true, in an amazing adventure and much more than that too.

I had seen talking penguins, and flown without props, and I had explored the cave of Santa Clops!

Santa Clops!
Dino-penguins that fly!
The cave!
That was amazing!
said the kids with a cry.
Goodbye Mr. Bones!
Merry Christmas to you!
Same to you children, and be careful what you do.

Printed in Great Britain
by Amazon

32793791R00025